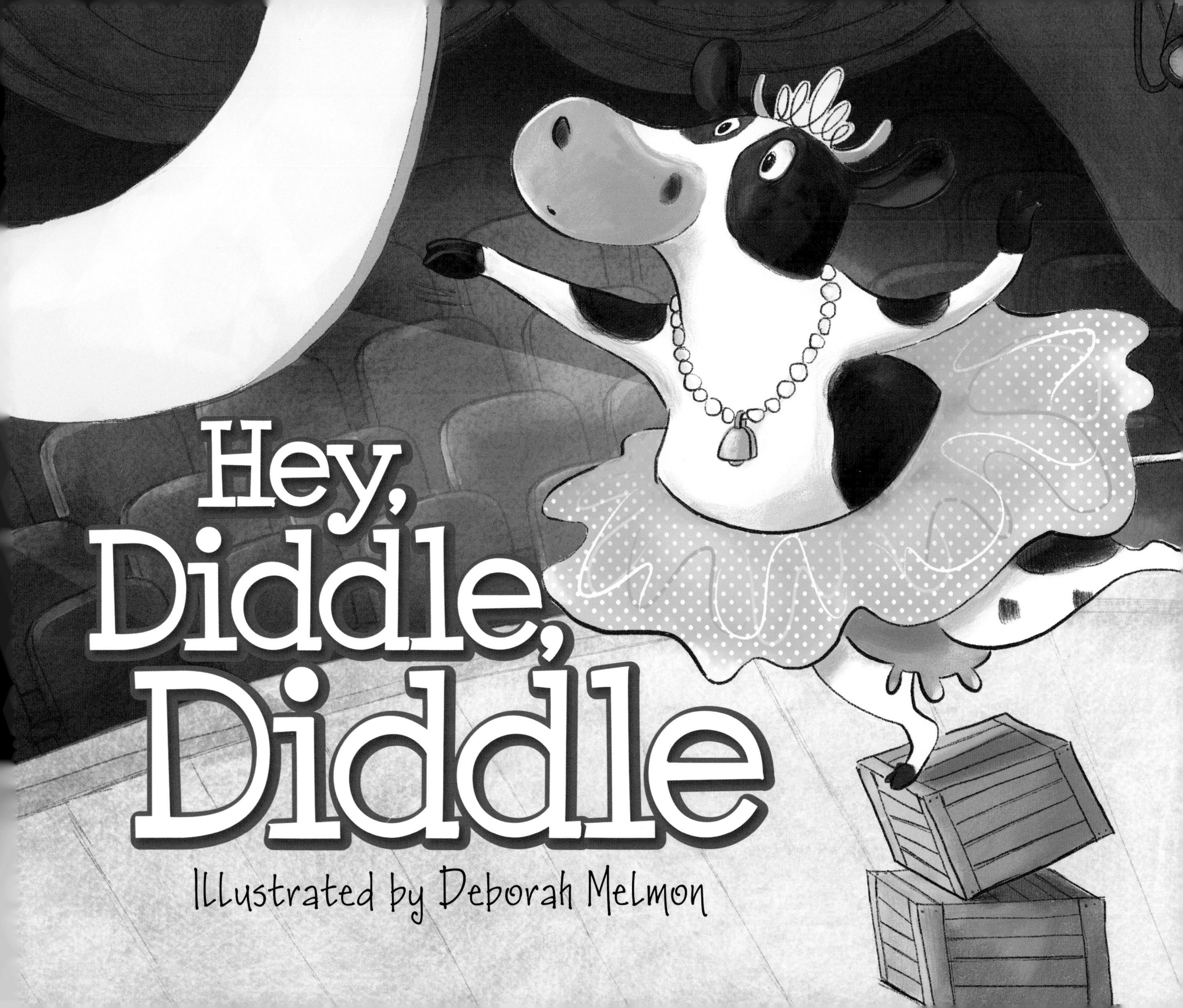

Hey, Diddle, Diddle

Illustrated by Deborah Melmon

ISBN 978-0-9897814-4-2
Printed in Mexico on FSC® paper
from well-managed forests

Music Together LLC
174 Nassau Street #340
Princeton NJ 08542
www.musictogether.com
(800) 728-2692

MUSIC TOGETHER®

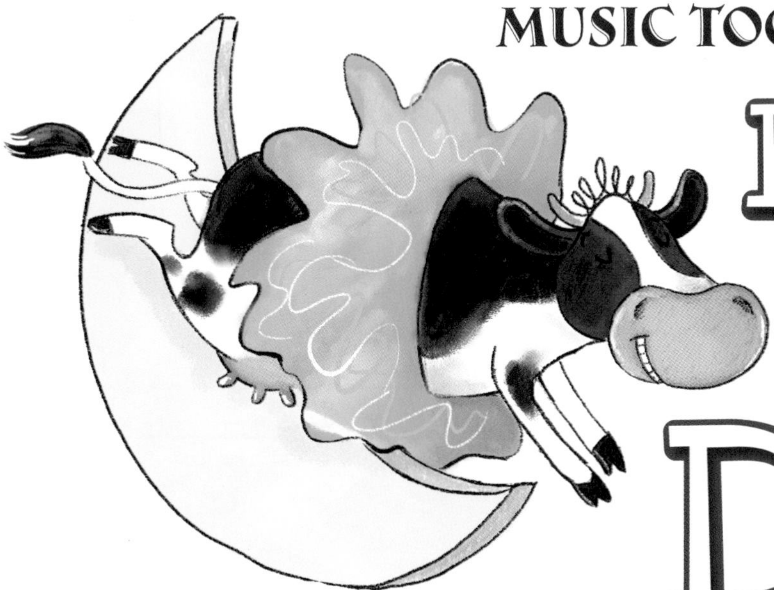

Hey, Diddle, Diddle

Welcome

Since 1987, Music Together has been bringing the Joy of Family Music® to young children and their families. This Singalong Storybook offers a new way to enjoy one of our best-loved Music Together songs. We invite you to sing it, read it, and use it as a starting point for conversation and imaginative play with your child.

Using the Book

If you're a Music Together family, you might start singing as soon as you turn the pages. But even if you've never attended one of our classes, you and your child can have hours of fun and learning with this Singalong Storybook. Read the story and enjoy the illustrations with your child, and then try some of the suggested activities that follow. The book can also help inspire artwork or enhance pre-literacy skills. You can even invent your own variations of the story or involve the whole family in some musical dramatic play.

Using the Recording Of course, using the recording to learn the song will enhance your enjoyment of the book. See page 31 for ways to get the Singalong Storybook songs and see the video "Using Your Singalong Storybook Musically." Or, if you play an instrument such as piano or guitar, you'll find it easy to pick out the song using the music page at the end of the book.

Hey, diddle, diddle, the cat and the fiddle,

The cow jumped over the moon — yeah!

The little dog laughed to see such sport,

And the dish ran away with the spoon—yeah!

The dish ran away with the spoon!

Hey, diddle, diddle,
The cat and the fiddle,
The cow jumped over the moon—yeah!

MOON JUMP

The little dog laughed to see such sport,

MOON JUMP
DRESS
REHEARSAL

And the dish ran away with the spoon—yeah!

The dish ran away with the spoon!

Hey, diddle, diddle, the cat and the fiddle,

The cow jumped over the moon—yeah!

The little dog laughed
to see such sport,

And the dish ran away with the spoon—yeah!
The dish ran away with the spoon—yeah!

The dish ran away
with the spoon—yeah!
The dish ran away
with the spoon!

Activities

Surprise!

Your child will love bouncing rhythmically on your lap as you sing the song. Create a surprise with a quick change of movement on each "yeah!"—lift your child high, lean him back, tickle her tummy. Repeat one surprise for a while; then try others and enjoy your child's responses.

Invent Verses

Sing about your child: "Hey, Diddle, Diddle, Celeste and her fiddle, her mommy jumped over the moon..." Or sing your child's ideas: What else might the cat play? What else could the cow jump over? It doesn't have to rhyme — and the sillier, the better!

Jazz Band

Get out your own non-breakable dishes, spoons, and other kitchen stuff, and have fun jamming along to the recording of the song. Try taking turns playing a pot or pan solo during the instrumental section.

Literacy

This story is filled with a colorful array of characters and scenes. As you sing or read through with your child, take turns pointing out what the cow is doing on each page. How does she feel? How about the cat? The fiddle? Follow any of the six main characters through the story, and have fun guessing what they might be doing, thinking, and feeling—even when they don't appear on the page.

Get Up and Move!

Dance any way you like, or do movements that go with the song. Imitate a cat playing a fiddle, swing your child through the air as the cow jumps over the moon, tickle a tummy when the dog laughs, and run across the room like the dish and the spoon. And it's fun to stop suddenly for a moment and FREEZE on each "yeah!"

Discussion

The cow—and other characters in the story—had to have determination and persistence to finally achieve a successful moon jump. What did they experience and feel along the way? What does it mean to "try, try, again"?

Hey, Diddle, Diddle

Music by K. Guilmartin
Words by Mother Goose

About the Song

The true origins of "Hey, Diddle, Diddle" are mysterious. Some say inspiration came from celestial constellations, while others believe the rhyme references a 16th century English queen. Still others say that "Hey, Diddle, Diddle" has no real meaning—it's just a pleasantly silly tale. Whatever the real story, children are just as drawn to it today as they were in 1765, when it was first published in "Tales of Mother Goose."

Music Together has turned "Hey, Diddle, Diddle" into a jazzy song that offers a fresh twist on this centuries-old rhyme. Children love moving to its lively rhythms and freezing in place on each "yeah!" It's also a terrific song for swing dancing, so grab a partner and dance along!

About Music Together®

Music Together classes offer a wide range of activities that are designed to be engaging and enjoyable for children from birth through age seven. By presenting a rich tonal and rhythmic mix as well as a variety of musical styles, Music Together provides children with a depth of experience that stimulates and supports their growing music skills and understanding.

Developed by Founder/Director Kenneth K. Guilmartin and his coauthor, Director of Research Lili M. Levinowitz, Ph.D., Music Together is built on the idea that all children are musical, that their parents and caregivers are a vital part of their music learning, and that their natural music abilities will flower and flourish when they are provided with a sufficiently rich learning environment.

And it's fun! Our proven methods not only help children learn to embrace and express their natural musicality—they often help their grateful grownups recapture a love of music, too. In Music Together classes all over the world, children and their families learn that music can happen anywhere, every day, at any time of the day—and they learn they can make it themselves.

Known worldwide for our mixed-age family classes, we have also adapted our curriculum to suit the needs of infants, older children, and children in school settings such as preschools, kindergartens, and early elementary grades. Visit www.musictogether.com to see video clips of Music Together classes; read about the research behind the program; purchase instruments, CDs, and books; and find a class near you. Keep singing!

Getting the Music

There is a download card for the song "Hey, Diddle, Diddle" in the front of this book; or at www.musictogether.com/storybooks you can listen to the song anytime. You can also find it on the award-winning Music Together CD **Family Favorites® 2**. CDs and downloads are available from Music Together, iTunes, and Amazon. To get the most out of your storybook, see the video **"Using Your Singalong Storybook Musically"** on our website.

The Family Favorites® 2 CD includes 19 songs and a 32-page booklet with many family activities to enjoy.

Come visit us at **www.musictogether.com.**

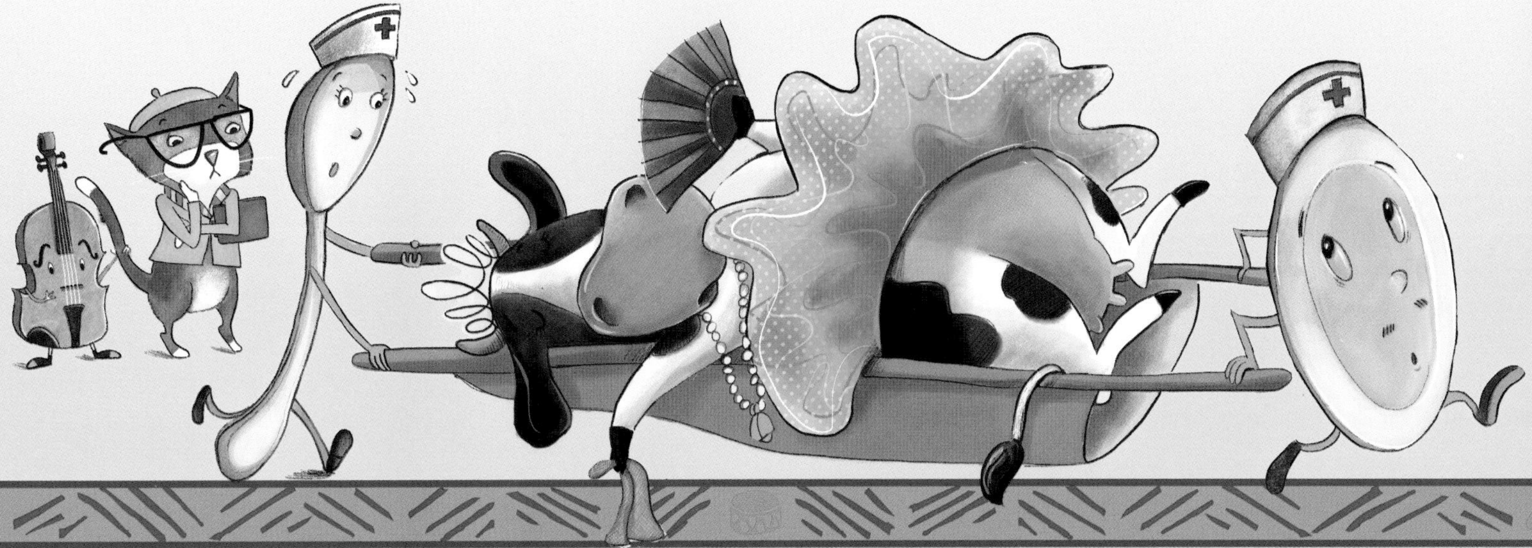

Music Together LLC

Kenneth K. Guilmartin, Founder/Director

Catherine Judd Hirsch, Director of Publishing and Marketing

Marcel Chouteau, Manager of Production and Distribution

Jill Bronson, Manager of Retail and Market Research

Susan Pujdak Hoffman, Senior Editor

Kate Battenfeld, Devi Borton, Linda Brasaemle, Contributing Writers

Developed by Q2A/Bill Smith, New York, NY